# DISNEY'S TARZAN

Adapted by Justine Korman

Illustrated by Len Smith, Denise Shimabukuro
Painted by Andrea & John Alvin

Cover illustration by Judith Clarke, Denise Shimabukuro
Painted by Andrea & John Alvin

## 🍎 A GOLDEN BOOK • NEW YORK

Golden Books Publishing Company, Inc., New York, New York 10106

One stormy night, near the coast of Africa, a man rowed his family away from a sinking ship. Soon the family reached the shore of a nearby island. There the parents built a tree house to shelter themselves and their baby boy.

No other humans lived in this part of the world. But there were plenty of animal families in the jungle.

One day an ape named Kala was lagging behind as her family moved through the jungle. Kala was very sad. She had lost her baby to the apes' great enemy, Sabor the leopard.

Just then Kala heard the cry of another baby and followed the sound to the tree house. One look around told her that the evil Sabor had visited this place, too.

Kala knew that the tiny creature she'd found needed care. She gently scooped him up in her strong arms.

When Kala returned home, the other apes stared at the human baby. "What is that freaky-lookin' thing?" hooted a young ape named Terk. "He's a baby," Kala said. "I'm going to be his mother now." Then she gently placed the tiny baby in Terk's arms.

"He is not like us," Kerchak, the gorilla leader, objected. "I cannot let you put our family in danger. You have to take him back!"

But Kala already loved this baby, and she finally convinced Kerchak to let her keep the infant. She named him Tarzan.

One day when Tarzan was five, he accidentally caused an elephant stampede. The ape family almost got trampled. Angry, Kerchak told Kala that Tarzan would never fit in.

Tarzan was upset by Kerchak's anger. And he was sad because he was so different from the other apes.

Kala understood Tarzan's distress. Gently, she showed him that they were the same inside. That was what really mattered.

Tarzan was determined to prove himself to Kerchak. He wanted to be the best ape ever. From the hippos he learned how to swim. From the monkeys he learned how to swing on vines. From the rhino's horn, he got the idea for a special tool—a spear.

One day Kerchak fought a great battle with Sabor. The killer leopard was about to win when Tarzan came to the rescue.

His spear broke, but Tarzan was now strong and clever. He defeated Sabor and saved Kerchak.

The apes cheered! Kala was very proud. At last Kerchak was ready to accept Tarzan as part of the ape family.

Suddenly the jungle echoed with a terrible new noise—gunshots! Kerchak led his family to safety. But Tarzan was curious. He hurried to see what had made the thunderlike sound.

Tarzan was shocked to see three creatures who looked so much like him. The "creatures" were Professor Porter, his daughter Jane, and their guide, Clayton. The Porters had come to Africa to study gorillas.

Almost immediately, Jane got into trouble with some
baboons. Tarzan swung to the rescue! Suddenly Jane was
flying through the jungle in the strong arms of someone
who could speak to the baboons in their own language!

Tarzan also wanted to speak to Jane. He pointed at himself and said, "Tar-zan."

At first Jane didn't realize that this was Tarzan's name. But she finally understood, and told Tarzan her name. Tarzan gently took Jane's chin in his hand and said, "Jane."

Kerchak ordered Tarzan to stay away from the strange,
noisy creatures. But Tarzan was curious about them.
At the human camp Tarzan learned many things.

Then he found out that the Porters would be going home very soon.

Clayton saw that Tarzan had strong feelings for Jane.

"If Jane sees gorillas, she stays?" Tarzan asked. Slyly Clayton nodded yes.

So Tarzan asked his friends Terk and Tantor, the elephant, to distract Kerchak while he brought the humans to see the gorillas.

The baby apes loved Jane! Tarzan taught her to say, "Jane
stays with Tarzan," in the gorillas' language.

Suddenly Terk and Tantor crashed through the bushes with
Kerchak close behind. Tarzan held the powerful ape back so
the humans could escape.

Kerchak was furious. "You betrayed us all!" he roared at Tarzan.

At that point, Kala made a decision. She took Tarzan to the tree house so he could learn about his past and make a choice—did he belong with the apes or with the humans?

Tarzan followed his heart to Jane.

Terk and Tantor watched their friend leave. "Go on, you bald ingrate!" Terk shouted, but she was more sad than angry.

Once on board the ship, Tarzan had a nasty surprise:
Clayton and his greedy henchmen had taken over. The Porters
were already prisoners.

Soon, in spite of his great strength, Tarzan was a captive, too!
When he learned that Clayton planned to capture the apes,
Tarzan let out a wild cry.

Back on shore Terk and Tantor heard their friend. They knew immediately that Tarzan was in trouble and rushed to his rescue.

As soon as he was free, Tarzan raced off to save his gorilla family from Clayton. Jane and Porter joined Tarzan's animal friends to help.

Clayton heard the rescuers coming. "Take all the apes you
can back to the boat," he ordered his men. "I'm going hunting!"

Suddenly Kerchak charged in front of Tarzan just as Clayton fired his rifle. Kerchak fell. Tarzan finally defeated Clayton, but Kerchak was dying. "Forgive me," Tarzan begged the great ape.

Kerchak knew that he'd been wrong when he told Kala that Tarzan wouldn't fit in. "I misjudged you," he said. "Our family will look to you now. Take care of them, my son."

The next morning, the Porters were ready to leave.

"I will miss you, Jane," Tarzan said. Jane got into the boat,
but her heart really was with Tarzan.

"You love him," her father said.

Jane knew it was true. She jumped into the water and ran
back to Tarzan.

Tarzan was happy that Jane had chosen to remain with him. Her father was happy, too. He would stay in Africa studying the gorillas who so fascinated him.

Together they headed into the jungle with the ape family where they would all live happily ever after.